Slinky Dog © POOF-Slinky, LLC

Mr. and Mrs. Potato Head® and Tinkertoys® are registered trademarks of Hasbro, Inc. Used with permission. © Hasbro, Inc. All rights reserved.

Mattel and FisherPrice toys used with permission. © Mattel, Inc. All rights reserved.

Copyright © 2018 Disney Enterprises, Inc., and Pixar.

For information, address Disney Press, 1200 Grand Central Avenue, Glendale, California 91201.

ISBN 978-1-368-04045-7
Printed in China
First Slipcase Edition, August 2018
10 9 8 7 6 5 4 3 2 1

For more Disney Press fun, visit www.disneybooks.com

TOY STORY 3

Disney PRESS

Los Angeles • New York

Andy loved his toys, and they loved him. Sheriff Woody, Buzz Lightyear, Jessie the cowgirl, Rex, Hamm, and all the rest were happiest when they were off on one of Andy's wildly imaginative adventures. It didn't matter whether Andy pretended the toys had X-ray vision or superhuman strength, or whether he made them villains or heroes. The toys all agreed: simply being played with by a kid—by Andy—was the best feeling in the world.

But as Andy grew into a teenager, he played with the toys less and less. By the time he was preparing for college, the toys were very worried. What would happen to them? Woody tried to reassure everyone. Andy would just tuck them all in the attic for safekeeping, he explained.

Andy's mom had another idea, however. She suggested that Andy donate his old toys to a daycare center.

"No one's going to want those," he told her. "They're junk."

The toys were shocked. Then, Andy opened the toy box, scooped up Rex, Hamm, Slinky, and Mr. and Mrs. Potato Head—and dumped them into a garbage bag! He paused for a moment, looking at his two favorites, Buzz and Woody. Then he dropped Woody into a box marked COLLEGE—and Buzz went into the garbage bag, too!

At first, the toys thought they were headed for the garbage can. But in fact, Andy planned to put the bag in the attic. Then Andy's mom made a terrible mistake. She assumed the bag was trash and dumped it at the curb.

Frantic, Woody climbed out the window to help his friends. He was still looking for them when the garbage truck arrived. He watched in horror as the trash collector hurled the bags into the back of the truck and crushed the entire load with the compactor!

Then Woody noticed an upside-down recycling bin moving across Andy's driveway. His friends had escaped!

Inside the garage, the toys were hurt and confused. What would they do now that Andy had thrown them away?

Jessie had an idea: go to the daycare center! She convinced everyone to climb inside the box of old toys that Mrs. Davis planned to donate.

Woody followed his friends into the box. He tried to explain about the garbage bag mix-up, but the toys didn't believe him.

SLAM! Suddenly, Andy's mom shut the hatchback, got in, and started driving.

Soon the receptionist at Sunnyside Daycare was carrying the box of toys down to the daycare center's Butterfly Room.

While the children were playing, Andy's toys couldn't contain their excitement and spilled out onto the floor. The daycare toys welcomed them with open arms.

Friendliest of all was a big, pink bear who smelled like strawberries. "Welcome to Sunnyside!" he called warmly. "I'm Lots-o'-Huggin' Bear! But please, call me Lotso!"

"Mr. Lotso," asked Rex, "do toys here get played with every day?"

"All day long," Lotso answered. "When the kids get old, new ones come in. No owners means no heartbreak."

To the toys, daycare was sounding better and better!

Lotso and a doll named Big Baby led the toys on a tour of Sunnyside before escorting them to their new home at the center: the Caterpillar Room.

Woody begged his friends not to stay. They belonged at Andy's house.

But Jessie and the others disagreed. "We can have a new life here, Woody," the cowgirl argued.

Woody could see his friends' minds were made up. Feeling sad and conflicted, he said goodbye.

He clambered onto the roof and used an old kite to propel himself over the daycare center's walls. When he crash-landed a little while later, he was bruised, hatless, and dangling by his pull string from a tree branch.

The receptionist's daughter, Bonnie, ran over to the dangling cowboy and shoved him into her backpack. Then she took him home.

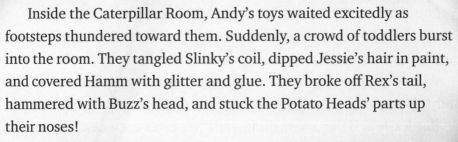

Inside the Caterpillar Room, Andy's toys waited excitedly as footsteps thundered toward them. Suddenly, a crowd of toddlers burst into the room. They tangled Slinky's coil, dipped Jessie's hair in paint, and covered Hamm with glitter and glue. They broke off Rex's tail, hammered with Buzz's head, and stuck the Potato Heads' parts up their noses!

One of the toddlers threw Buzz onto a windowsill. He could see into the Butterfly Room . . . where a group of four- and five-year-olds were playing gently with Lotso and the other daycare toys.

Buzz wondered: Why had Andy's toys been put in the Caterpillar Room? The toddlers played too rough!

After the children went home, the toys tried to put themselves
back together.

"Andy never played with us like that!" Rex exclaimed.

"I'll go talk to Lotso about moving us to the other room,"
said Buzz.

While he was gone, Mrs. Potato Head started to see strange images,
coming to her through an eye she'd lost back at Andy's house.

"Andy's looking in the attic," she said. "Why is he so upset?"
She gasped. "I think he did mean to put us in the attic!"

Now that the toys realized their mistake, they knew they had to
go home!

Buzz found some of the Sunnyside toys inside a vending machine in the teacher's lounge. He overheard them talking—and learned that these toys knew how dangerous the Caterpillar Room was. Andy's toys had been sent there on purpose! Buzz tried to go and warn his friends, but he was captured.

When Lotso arrived, he was as friendly as ever. He even granted Buzz's request to be transferred to the Butterfly Room—on the condition that Buzz's friends stay behind.

"I can't accept," said Buzz. "We're a family. We stay together."

Suddenly, Lotso's attitude changed. With a cruel smile, he called for the Buzz Lightyear instruction manual. Then he ordered his gang to reset Buzz's switch to demo mode.

When Lotso arrived in the Caterpillar Room, Andy's toys begged
to leave.

"Here's the thing," the bear said, grinning nastily. "You ain't leaving
Sunnyside." He wanted Andy's toys to stay with the littlest kids.
Somebody had to endure their rough play, and it wasn't going to be
Lotso's gang!

Then, suddenly, Buzz appeared and accused his old friends of being
"minions of Zurg"!

Jessie and the others were shocked. What had happened to Buzz?

Lotso's gang herded Andy's toys into the room's wire cubbies. When
Mr. Potato Head fought back, Big Baby made him stay overnight in a
covered sandbox out in the playground.

Lotso chuckled and left, leaving the captives under Buzz's stern
guard. The happy daycare had turned into a grim prison!

Meanwhile, at Bonnie's house, Woody was actually having fun. The little girl had a great imagination, and her toys were very kind.

But then Woody discovered he was just a few streets from Andy's house!

"If you guys ever get to Sunnyside Daycare," said Woody, waving goodbye, "tell them Woody made it home."

The toys gasped. Chuckles, a toy clown, knew all about Sunnyside. Long ago, Chuckles explained, he, Lotso, and Big Baby had belonged to a little girl named Daisy. One day, the toys were accidentally left behind during a trip. Lotso led them on a long journey home, but Daisy had already gotten a new pink bear. Heartbroken and furious, Lotso ripped off the pendant with Daisy's name on it that Big Baby always wore. Eventually, the trio ended up at Sunnyside, where Lotso became the daycare center's bitter tyrant. Chuckles would have perished, except that Bonnie rescued him after he was broken.

As much as Woody wanted to get home to Andy, he knew he couldn't leave his friends in Lotso's clutches. The next day, he hitched a ride to the daycare center in Bonnie's backpack.

The cowboy found his pals and told them how they could break out of Sunnyside. That night, the toys sprang into action. Woody and Slinky surprised the toy monkey sitting by the security monitors and grabbed the daycare keys. Mr. Potato Head distracted Big Baby while the others captured Buzz. Meanwhile, Barbie forced Ken to tell her about Buzz's instruction manual. Then she and the other toys attempted to reset Buzz's switch—but something went wrong. Now Buzz only spoke Spanish!

Despite the setback, everyone made it to their destination: the garbage chute in the playground.

Woody and the rest of the toys climbed
into the garbage chute and slid down
one by one. At the bottom, Slinky
formed a bridge between
the chute and the lid
of the nearby bin so
his friends could
walk across to
freedom.

But suddenly, Lotso
appeared. "Why don't you come
back and join our family again?"
he asked the toys.

"You're a liar and a bully, and
I'd rather rot in this bin than join
any family of yours!" Jessie replied.

Lotso scowled. "I didn't throw
you away," he replied. "Your kid did.
There isn't one kid who ever loved a
toy, really."

"What about Daisy?" Woody asked suddenly. "She lost you. By accident. She loved you!"

"She never loved me!" Lotso exploded angrily. "She left me!"

Big Baby's eyes filled with tears as he thought about Daisy.

"You want your mommy back? She never loved you!" Lotso shouted, and gave Big Baby a shove.

Big Baby had had enough. He hoisted Lotso into the air—and threw him into a big trash bin!

The daycare toys cheered. Things would be different at Sunnyside from now on.

"Come on! Hurry!" cried Woody, starting across the lid. He could hear a garbage truck rumbling toward them!

The toys followed, and climbed to safety on a wall.

Then Woody saw an Alien caught between the bin's lids. The cowboy ran back, but Lotso reached up and yanked Woody inside! The rest of Andy's toys jumped onto the lid and tried to pry it open, but the garbage truck lifted the container and tilted it upside down. Soon all the toys fell into the back of the truck.

The truck rumbled forward, then lurched to a stop. More trash rained down on them, and a TV landed on top of Buzz. Incredibly, the blow turned him back into his old self!

Soon the truck arrived at the Tri-County Landfill and dumped its load.

"The claaaaw!" shouted the Aliens excitedly as they toddled off toward a crane in the distance.

Woody tried to go after them but was cut off by a huge bulldozer. Rumbling, it pushed him and his friends toward an open pit.

The toys fell onto a conveyor belt that led to a shredder. But they soon discovered another conveyor belt above them that was magnetic. They grabbed on to whatever metal trash they could find and were lifted to safety.

Suddenly, they heard a cry for help. Lotso was trapped! Woody and Buzz dropped down and used a golf club to free him. The shredder was just inches away!

Woody grabbed Lotso's paw, the golf club flew toward the magnet, and all three were lifted to safety. Next they dropped down to their friends, who were on another conveyor belt far below.

They thought they saw daylight at the end of this belt, but suddenly realized it was actually an incinerator!

Lotso managed to find the emergency stop button that could save them all, but instead of pushing it, he hesitated. Then a cruel smirk came across his face, and he ran off.

Woody and his friends tumbled toward the fire, determined to face it the best way they knew how: together.

Then, suddenly, a large shadow passed
over them. A giant crane lowered its jaws and
scooped the toys up and away from the scorching fire. Inside the crane's
cab, the Aliens steered their friends over the landfill and dropped them
gently to the ground.

Now the toys had to get Woody home before Andy left for college.
Luckily, they spotted their neighborhood garbage man nearby, just
climbing into his truck. The toys hurried forward, ready to hitch
a ride home.

Lotso found his way onto a different truck. But he wouldn't be
hopping off anytime soon—he had been strapped to the front of it!

Woody and the gang arrived home as Andy was loading up the car. They had made it just in time!

Woody headed for a box marked COLLEGE, while the others climbed into an ATTIC box. Before they separated, Woody and Buzz shook hands.

"You know where to find us, cowboy," Buzz said.

Inside the COLLEGE box, Woody looked at a photo of Andy with all his toys. The cowboy knew that no matter where any of them went, they would always carry the memories of their time together. But as he sat in the box alone, something did not feel quite right.

Suddenly, Woody had an idea. He jumped out of the box, hastily wrote something on a sticky note, and placed it on the attic box.

When Andy arrived to grab the last boxes, he read the note. Then he opened the attic box and got a wonderful surprise—his toys hadn't been thrown away after all!

"Hey, Mom," he shouted. "Do you really think I should donate these?"

"It's up to you," she called back.

A little while later, Andy pulled up to Bonnie's house.

"Someone told me you're really good with toys," Andy said to the little girl.

As Andy introduced his toys to Bonnie, he was startled to find Woody in the box. He wasn't supposed to be there!

"My cowboy!" Bonnie cried happily.

Though it was hard for him, Andy let Woody stay with Bonnie, too. From the hug she gave the cowboy, Andy could see that she already loved him.

Back in the car, Andy took one last look at a smiling Bonnie surrounded by his toys.

"Thanks, guys," he said quietly before pulling away.

Bonnie went inside for lunch, and the toys watched Andy disappear down the street.

"So long, partner," said Woody.

Buzz and the others gathered around him. Their life with Andy was ending, but their adventures with Bonnie had just begun.